BABA?
Answer me!

Habibti,*
it's too late!
Protect yourself!

BABA!
NOOO!!

Sokar, habibti.
Listen to me.
You're the only
one who can
save us!

But I can't leave
you behind! The flames
are so high!

Go on ahead and get help!
Find your daredevil cousins, Rachid and Sa'id.
I'll wait here where it's safe, with Tifo and
the others, until you return.

4

* "SWEETHEART" OR "SWEETIE" WHEN SPEAKING TO A FEMALE (ARABIC)

LOWRIDERS
to the RESCUE

By
CATHY CAMPER

Illustrated by
RAÚL THE THIRD

IT WAS A WARM FALL DAY, AND AT THE LOWRIDERS IN SPACE GARAGE, EVERYONE WAS HARD AT WORK.

LUPE IMPALA, THE BEST MECHANIC IN TOWN, WAS WORKING ON A HOMEWORK ASSIGNMENT FOR HER COMMUNITY COLLEGE CLASS ENGINOLOGY 101, RECALIBRATING HOOLIWONKERS ON A CATALYTIC CONVERTER.

* THE MONARCH BUTTERFLIES

ARTIST AND MOSQUITO ELIRIO MALARIA WAS PAINTING MAGNIFICENT PINSTRIPING WITH HIS BEAK ON THE SIDE OF A CARGO VAN.

Sí,* usually they arrive around Día de los Muertos.** But the smell of smoke is in the air, even down here . . .

AND EL CHAVO FLAPJACK OCTOPUS DEL MAR JUNIOR WAS POLISHING THE CHROME UNDERSIDE OF THE UNDERSIDERS' CARRO . . .***

NO, WAIT, HE'S NOT THERE . . .

* YES   ** DAY OF THE DEAD   *** CAR

11

UM, FLAPJACK WAS WASHING THE RENTAL CAR FLEET. . . . ¡HÍJOLE!* HE'S NOT THERE EITHER! GENIE, HAVE YOU SEEN FLAPPY?

* JEEZ! WOW!

OH, THERE *HE* IS!

AHEM.

AND HERE WE HAVE EL CHAVO FLAPJACK OCTOPUS DEL MAR JUNIOR, THE BEST CAR WASHER AND BUFFER AND ... BUBBLE BLOWER? SIGH ... ALL IN ONE BUCKET!

Burbujas,* burbujas ... I'm the best at blowing bubbles! ¡Hola,** Genie!

Whoa! Who's that? It's a beautiful woman! She's dancing!

... and she's waving at ME!!

Maybe she heard my singing!

Ooo, Genie, I have a huge, gigantic crush on her! What should I do? I want to meet her, but I'm too shy!

* BUBBLES ** HI

* A GIRLFRIEND ** COME ON!

* A SAILOR

18

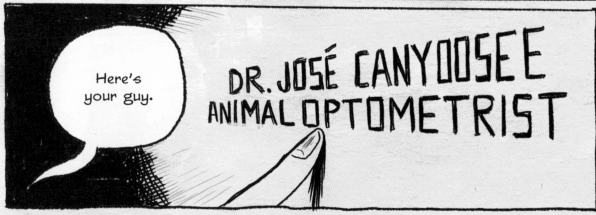

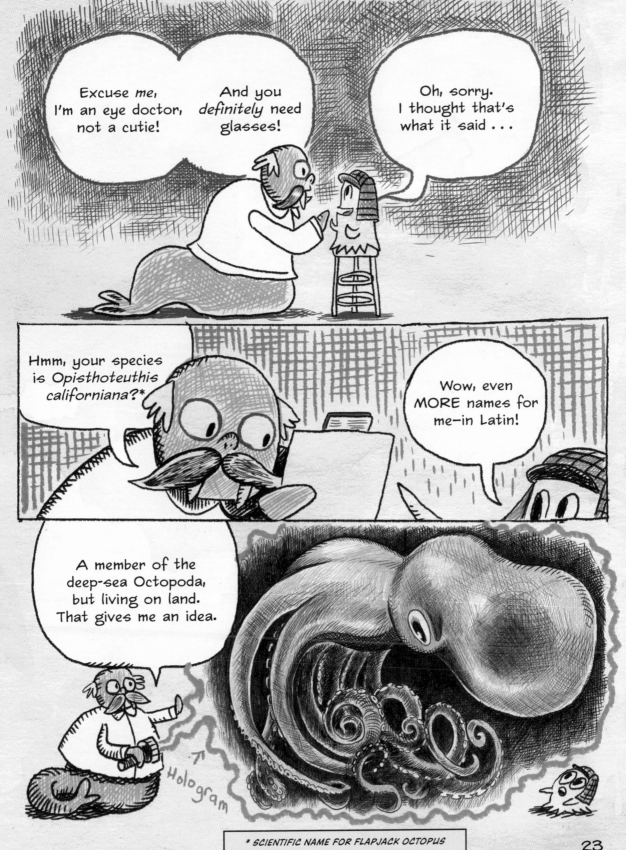

* SCIENTIFIC NAME FOR FLAPJACK OCTOPUS

23

* DUDES, GUYS

Wire rim?

Demasiado pequeños.*

Horn-rimmed?

Demasiado grandes.**

Or rhinestone, para ocasiones especiales?***

Maybe I need them all!

* TOO SMALL ** TOO BIG *** FOR SPECIAL OCCASIONS

* LITTLE ONE

29

That's not quite what I expected . . .

They look good, El Chavo!

Impressive! You look so smart!

Wear them until your eyes adjust. You won't need them forever.

It's great being able to see!

Let's go to Ojos de Búho* for a snack.

Whoa, a stop sign! I didn't know they were so red!

¡Qué chido es poder ver!**

* OWL EYES ** IT'S SO COOL TO BE ABLE TO SEE!

* GET OUT!

** MIGRATORY INSECTS

* PEACE! (AN ARABIC GREETING) ** WELCOME!

That is so sad.

No, you're the first mariposa we've seen. We've been worried about all of you.

My family was safe when I left them. But I guess no one can get through the flames right now.

YOUR TABLE IS READY, LUPE ALPACA.

AUGH! I'M AN IMPALA!

We'll help you rescue them as soon as it's safe.

Inshallah, that would be wonderful!

Wow, she's gone through so much! Will she even talk to me?

IMPALA? LIKE THE CAR?

¡Hola! ¿Qué tal?*

?

Oh, I get it! The translation's down here!

* HI! HOW'S IT GOING?

40

* MARSHMALLOW SALAD

Thanks, I'm starving! Most of the wildflower and milkweed patches where we'd eat got paved over or killed by weed killers.

Your drinks. Care for straws?

No, thanks.

That's a cool straw!

SLURP SLURP

I—um, we— want to help you out, however we can.

Aww, Flappy, that's so—

YUM!

HA HA HA HA

43

How 'bout you hang out with us? We run the Lowriders in Space garage here in town. I'm Lupe, the mechanic; that's Elirio, he paints the carros; and you've met El Chavo Flapjack. He buffs and cleans things.

I'm Sokar. I'm so happy to meet you all!

¡Qué chido!*

I was so thirsty! Shukran!**

What language is that?

44

* HOW COOL! ** THANK YOU! (ARABIC)

* POPSICLES ** KOREAN FORM OF MARTIAL ARTS

And this big hotel, that's El Cortez. Our city has many ancient Spanish names, going back at least to the Jurassic Era!

Ay, Flappy! He must know this city wasn't here with the dinosaurs?!

¡Oh, perdóname*! I forgot those humans were very rude to you!

No, it's okay.

* FORGIVE ME!

49

It's so silly, though. Look at the names of those snooty guys: Martínez, Sánchez, Cortez.

The "ez" in their names comes from Arabic, from the Moors in Spain! Thousands of Spanish words–like *aceituna*, from *zatun*, for olive, or *loco*, from *lakī*, for foolish–all come from Arabic words!

I wonder if those guys even know how much we have in common?

See these tiles near the fountain? That tile design comes from the Moors too.

Claro, that's true. These Talavera tiles look so much like ancient Islamic tiles!

And even my name, Sokar—what Spanish word does that remind you of?

It sounds like . . . azúcar, sugar.

Yup, both the English and the Spanish words come from Arabic! You're very smart!

Huh, that's wild!

51

53

* YIKES!

COMING NEXT MONTH! SUPER GIGANTE APTS. featuring 3 garages each! Rooftop firepits! New 6-lane boulevard on-ramp. MAKER SPACE CLOSETS! HERMANOS MARTINEZ —WHEELER DEALER

This is horrible! It'll ruin the beachfront! Even more than this ugly letrero . . . *

With this development, forget about sunlight and ocean access!

Three cars per unit? Six-lane on-ramp? That's so much pollution!

Maker Space closets? I'd rather have the Rec Center back!

zoning solo para humanos! **

Wait a sec, humans only? This isn't just bad for the neighborhood, it's unfair to us!

Look! Hidden down here, it says they need Señor Bufolardo's approval to build this—and his dinero.*

Hey! What if we could convince him to rebuild the Rec Center instead, and make it like it used to be?

The original Rec Center was for *everybody*. It was el corazón,** the lifeblood of our neighborhood. We could bring that back.

YES!

It wouldn't hurt to try. We go way back with him; we still have his phone number.

* MONEY ** THE HEART

Hello, Señor Bufolardo?

Sí, diga.*

It's Lupe, from **LOWRIDERS** in **SPACE**. I'm calling about those Súper-Hiper-Gigante** Apartment buildings you might be funding?

While she's on the phone, let me show you around . . .

Well, we thought it would be better if you would save the Rec Center instead! *Everyone* could use it, and it would improve the barrio . . . ***

* YES, TELL ME ** SUPER-HYPER-GIANT *** NEIGHBORHOOD

There are our garage bays, there's my bowling ball, here's my *favorite* books . . .

Sorry, mis amigos,* but the Upscale Business Association wants the new apartment residents to become their future customers. If you want me to fund the Rec Center, you will need to convince me— and *them*—that it's a smart use of our dinero.

What do you mean?

You Lowriders are inventive: *Show* me how you'd renovate the place. Prove that it would generate money for the barrio. You got until the end of the month.

Hmm.

. . . Sokar, here's our prized possession. I bet you've never seen *this* before . . .

* MY FRIENDS

AUUGH! She doesn't like me! SHE HATES ME! I blew it!

Oh, Flappy. I'm sorry. I have a feeling she'll be back. Don't lose hope just yet.

Love's tough when you got tres corazones!*

So what? Who cares? Sokar will never speak to me again!

I talked to Bufolardo. There's a chance he'll go for the Rec Center remodel—but only if we have a plan the Business Association will support too. And THEY just want to make money.

Give her time. We'll help rescue her family when the wildfires die down. But right now, our old car can't handle all that soot in the air. No way will it fly.

* THREE HEARTS

So what? Even if we help her, she thinks I'm a polluter, a gas hog!

But what if I rebuilt our car engine so it's nonpolluting? That would impress her!

And ese,* what if we let you drive? The way to someone's heart is bajito y suavecito—with your car!

Yeah, right! I'm a wiggly, tentacled mess. I can't even see over the steering wheel!

We can put my Enginology textbook under your bucket.

72

* DUDE

Hmm. "For solar cars to work, the shape of the car must be aerodynamic and be able to fit the amount of cells needed."

SOLAR PANELS

Augh! Too bulky. Pepe will know what to do!

I'll get the parts now.

What's up? Pepe's is closing?!

¿Pepe, qué pasa?* Are you retiring?

GOING OUT OF BUSINESS

No, amiga, I wish! The casero** wants me out by next month, so they can tear this place down!

EVERYTHING MUST GO!

* WHAT'S HAPPENING? ** LANDLORD

* YES, IT'S TRUE ** I LOVE MY JOB! *** MANY THANKS

Speaking of the environment, how would I attach photocells and keep our car aerodynamic—like these instructions say?

Ah, photocells are old-school! Try this experimental solar cell paint!

Just paint it on; it's transparent! So Elirio's artwork won't be erased—and the paint absorbs solar energy!

I'd get the solar engine adapter kit too. The Aire Fresco* model is on sale, so is the paint, and I'll throw in the electrical connectors for free!

I'll take them all! Thanks, Pepe. I'll start customizing right away! And we'll think of something to stop this demolition.

I know you will!

* FRESH AIR

Our whole barrio's being destroyed. But what can we do?

I just talked to Pepe. In one month, they're tearing down his place and Ojos de Búho to build some polluting car factory instead!

¡Ay, nooo! First the Rec Center, now this? We have to stop them!

But how? It's all part of the Upscale Business Association's plan.

Wait a sec!

What if our plan not only saved the Rec Center, but it did something to save the environment too?

But how would that stop their construction?

We could turn the Rec Center into a community center: We could have classes, workshop space, community gardens, neighborhood events . . . and a churro* stand! We can get the community to support our plan, I know it!

Flappy, you're brilliant! The Upscale Business Association would have to support that!

New green businesses! ¡Buena idea!** I could clean out that vacant lot to grow wildflowers and organic plants.

I could convert cars to green technology! And I could start with our lowrider as a test!

Hmm. I'd like to invent something to stop the ocean from turning into plastic soup.

Well, keep working on it! You're full of good ideas, El Chavo.

Sí, you're a genius, Flappy.

Maybe if this green Rec Center works, Sokar will talk to me again.

That's it, Genie! Bubbles are the perfect containers! When we're done with them, we just pop or swallow them!

Elirio, what if Kooky Kola came in a bubble instead of a bottle?

Hmm. But what would keep the bubbles from bursting? And you're gonna need muchas burbujas, muchacho.*

Don't worry, I got that figured out: What's the best source of bubbles we know?

* LOTS OF BUBBLES, DUDE

Um . . . a bar of soap?

Hint. Hint.

No—betta fish make whole nests out of bubbles! My betta pals even invented a seaweed extract to make their bubbles stronger. Strong enough to hold liquid!

¡Ah, perfecto!*

The bettas agreed to blow the bubbles, and we'll hook up a spout to fill them with Kola.

You've already hooked me, Flappy!

Okay! I've retooled and solarized our car! If our plan works, I bet it'll keep Pepe in business.

Everyone will want his eco-friendly car parts too!

And El Cortez and Ojos de Búho can serve beverages in my Kooky Kola bubbles!

The Upscale Business Association could revamp themselves to be more green too.

* PERFECT!

* LET'S GET TO WORK!

We have an idea, and we have a space where we can make it happen. But we need more than just the four of us.

How do we get la comunidad* involved? Hey—I know who we can ask!

Sokar! She's an activist! Let's go to the forest and find her.

Are you coming, Flappy?

No way! I don't want to see her!

Fine, homes, but I think you're being muy sensible.**

MERCADO

* THE COMMUNITY ** VERY SENSITIVE

* I'M WORRIED

Over here we'll have drive-thru bays to solarize cars, and these sun patches will become an invernadero* for the little milkweed sprouts.

Of course, that's in addition to basketball courts, meeting rooms, underwater ping-pong, and a snack bar.

Wow. This looks amazing! Is there anything you guys can't fix?

If the barrio builds it, they'll all back it and benefit from it too!

And if the barrio turns out in support, the businesses would be smart to back it too.

* GREENHOUSE

89

I'll call Bufolardo now to make sure they all come to see it before they decide.

I'll distribute these!

engage animals people everyone! the REC ROOM

LOCO for LOCAL support the REC ROOM

SUPPORT the REC ROOM

SUPPORT the REC ROOM clean air initiative

support the

I'll help too! ¡Vamos! Every minute counts!

Sokar's so inspired!

I wonder if she knows it was all my idea?

I'd like manakeesh,* please.

Huh, taco al pastor is like shawarma, only with pork!

Chicken with mole, eight tacos, please, to go, ensalada de nopales, and frijoles refritos y pico de gallo . . .

¡Y salsa picante!

* ARABIC FLATBREAD TOPPED WITH ZA'ATAR AND GROUND MEAT

Our foods are . . .

iguales!*

nafssou!**

I bet back in the day, the Moors and the Spanish shared a lot of the spices and a lot of the same recipes.

Our ancestors ate GOOD!

Haha, high five for yummy food!

What if we combined our foods into new ones? Like a Morocco Taco . . . ***

* THE SAME ** THE SAME (LEBANESE-SYRIAN ARABIC) *** TORTILLA FOLDED IN HALF, FILLED WITH FOODS LIKE VEGETABLES, SEASONED MEAT, AND CHEESE

* STEAMED SEMOLINA SERVED WITH STEWS ** ARAB SALAD MADE OF PARSLEY, BULGUR (CRACKED WHEAT), MINT, TOMATOES, AND SOMETIMES CUCUMBER, WITH A DRESSING OF LEMON JUICE AND OLIVE OIL *** MASA (CORNMEAL DOUGH) CONTAINING BEANS OR SEASONED MEAT, WRAPPED IN CORNHUSKS AND STEAMED **** GRILLED CHICKEN ***** HA! HA! HA! ****** HA HA HA, AS TEXTED IN ARABIC

I'm giving Sokar a ride to find her family. *Tomorrow!* So NOW what am I gonna do?

But isn't that what you wanted?

I'm too short to drive, and my glasses aren't even listed on my license. But wait, where is my license? It's not in my wallet! BUT WAIT! I don't even *have* a license! How can I impress Sokar when I can't even drive?

¡Tranquilo,* Flappy! You don't need a license to drive in space. ¡Relájate! Estamos contigo.**

---

* CALM DOWN! ** RELAX! WE'RE WITH YOU

Now we can drive on two wheels . . .

FLIP!

Screech!!!

Hey, everyone! Flappy offered me a ride to rescue my family. Is that still okay?

But today is the day Señor Bufolardo and the Business Association are coming! They're going to show up—and we won't even be there!

The deadline is tomorrow—we can't let them tear down our barrio!

* ARABIC LETTER W, PRONOUNCED LIKE "WOW"

I know. But we made a promise. To our friend. It'll be okay. I know it will.

You're right. We gotta be there for Flappy. And maybe if we're lucky, we'll save the day TWICE—first up north, then for our barrio!

Okay, homes, Lupe customized your seat, so you can see. All you have to do is steer and flip the switches. They control the compressors on the wheels to make the car hop.

I dunno, will this work? Even if she loves our ride, I bet she thinks my glasses are ridículos.*

Pues . . .** I doubt she thinks that!

LORP!
BLURP!

Don't worry, El Chavo, you just need a little pomade on your flaps.

SLICK!

¿Eh, casanova? Next time Sokar sees you, she'll think you're el pulpo más guapo!***

O-KAY!!!

*RIDICULOUS **WELL . . . ***THE MOST HANDSOME OCTOPUS*

I got the milkweed ready to plant along the way!

We'll reestablish the Milkweed Motels so future butterflies will have lots of rest stops!

I'm worried! What if the Business Association and Bufolardo choose their plan over ours?

Have faith! Our work speaks for itself.

We'll argue our case with them when we get back.

¡Hola, Sokar! I, El Chavo Flapjack Octopus *Opisthoteuthis californiana* del Mar Junior would like to give you a ride in our newly revamped solar-powered ranfla!*

* LOWRIDER

108

Whew! So much loss! Nature can be so destructive!

Then again, fire makes room for new growth. Some seeds need wildfire to start to grow.

C-O-O-P

These Milkweed Motels will be there to welcome future butterflies. Shukran, Elirio!

Now, to find Mama and Tifo. I can't wait to see them.

Which direction?

Over there.

I told you I'd come back, Mama. I'm sorry it took me so long to figure out a way!

My new friends helped me, and I've been helping them.

We're trying to save the local Rec Center for the whole community. And there's room for all of you to stay until you're fully recovered.

We couldn't have done any of it without Sokar! She's made us all activists for the environment!

Sokar, that's amazing! Your baba would be so proud!

I haven't stopped thinking about him the whole time.

Yallah, Mama! I can't wait to show you!

Wait for us, habibti!

Your mama throws her chancla* at you? My mom does that to me all the time too!

Yeah, only mine calls hers a shabashib!**

HA! HA! HA! HA! HA!

Mariposas, hang tight!

Ay yi yi, Bufolardo and the Business Association will be there when we get back. We're flying from one wildfire into the next!

* FLIP-FLOP ** FLIP-FLOP (ARABIC)

We'll convert the engines here. Then cars drive through to the solar paint bays. I'm working on setting up the spray booths.

¿Y esto?

This is the lounge for our hard-working bettas!

And over here, free air and tire repairs, so folks can repair their own flats too! Servicio para todos.*

From now on, all my mechanics will train here!

What's that out there?

Elirio and Sokar are replanting wildflowers, árboles,** and organic food gardens. Nada mejor que aire fresco.***

* SERVICE FOR EVERYONE ** TREES *** NOTHING LIKE FRESH AIR

* AMAZING, RIGHT? ** YOU'VE USED YOUR CREATIVITY

I'd invest in recyclable tires like that! A much better plan than a car factory! Es muy buen negocio!*

If you make 'em, we'll test-drive 'em!

Plus the sap helps us monarchs. It gives us a poisonous alkaloid that we can eat, but which makes predators avoid us.

Didn't you ever wonder why our wings are so brightly colored? It's a warning that we're toxic.

¡Ja! ¡Ja! Your food is your secret ninja defense!

All very impressive! But what's this?

* IT'S VERY GOOD BUSINESS!

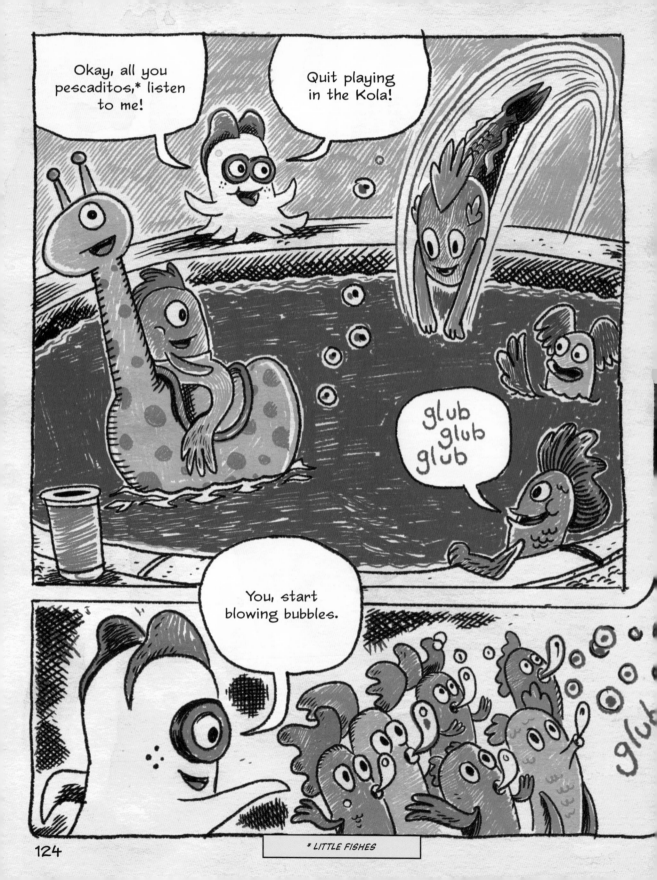

* LITTLE FISHES

* RIGHT NOW ** IT'S SPECTACULAR!

The Rec Center will be the pride of animals and people, todo el mundo!* By creating a sustainable city that cares about everyone equally—including Planet Earth—we'll make more money closer to HOME, which we can invest back into our community. That's good for all of us! ¡Bravo!

Everyone, the Rec Center is yours! We need all of our cooperation to keep our city—and the Earth—clean and green!

¡GRACIAS, Lowriders!

YAY! REC CENTER!

Support local economy

Also, I'd like to invite the monarchs to use the Rec Center just as we would, for as long as you need refuge! Hey Tifo, try this churro . . . ¿Sabroso, verdad?**

YUM YUM!

Shukran, Flapjack, you make us feel so welcome! You Lowriders came to the rescue—not just for us, but for the whole community.

whisper whisper whisper

whisper

On behalf of the Upscale Business Association, I'd like to offer an apology for how we've treated migrants. The Lowriders' welcoming behavior and Sokar's fresh new ideas put us to shame.

I accept your apology. I'm glad to help out.

One final announcement. It's high time we change the name of the Upscale Business Association to something more inclusive. Something that supports ALL local businesses.

I'd like to personally invite Pepe and Ojos de Búho to join as the inaugural members of the Barrio Business Association.

BARRIO BUSINESS ASSOCIATION

Hey, Sokar, wanna go for a ride solitos* just you and me?

Sure, Flappy! I love hanging out with you!

... And if you want, in a few months, I could even fly you back north again, to your home!

You're so sweet, Flappy, tan lindo!**

But the truth is, it takes generations of monarchs to complete our migration. When the seasons change again, Mom and I will fly north partway. Then Tifo and his generation will finish the flight to our homeland. My home is just my memory now.

* ALONE ** SO CUTE!

Uh-oh, Sokar . . . I wasn't paying attention. I'm lost! How do we get home?

Easy—follow the stars. From el norte,* go south. First Polaris, then the Big Dipper and Betelgeuse . . .

There's a star named Beetle Juice?!

It's Arabic! The ancient Arabs named lots of the stars. My baba taught me that.

If I could name a star, I'd name it after you. Mi estrellita.**

* THE NORTH ** MY LITTLE STAR

WHAT DOES IT MEAN? / ¿QUÉ SIGNIFICA?

¡a nosotros también!—and us too!

aceituna—olive

agua—water

ahora mismo—right now

Aire Fresco—Fresh Air

albi—my heart (Arabic)

Alex Plosivo—a pun on the Spanish word "explosivo," which means explosive

amigo, amiga—friend

¡Amo mi trabajo!—I love my job!

aquí esta el bulevar—here is the boulevard

árboles—trees

¡Ay chihuahua!—Yikes!

azúcar—sugar

baba—dad (Arabic)

bajito y suavecito—low and slow

barrio—neighborhood

basura—garbage

Betelgeuse—a red supergiant star in the constellation of Orion. In the 16th century, Arab astronomers called Orion the Giant (al-Juaza), so Betelgeuse (bet al-Juaza) means "the armpit of the giant"

¡Bienvenida!—Welcome!

¡Buena idea!—Good idea!

¡Buena suerte!—Good luck!

burbujas—bubbles

carro—car

casero—landlord

chancla—flip-flop

chica—girl

chida—cool

churro—fried pastry sprinkled with sugar and cinnamon

Cindy Nero—a pun on the Spanish "sin dinero," penniless or broke

claro—of course

couscous—steamed semolina served with stews

¡Cuatro!—Four!

cubeta—bucket

demasiado grandes—too big

demasiado pequeños—too small

Día de los Muertos—Day of the Dead

dinero—money

¿Dónde está tu amigo?—Where is your friend?

el corazón—the heart

el norte—the north

el pulpo más guapo—the most handsome octopus

ensalada de malvavisco—marshmallow salad

ensalada de nopales—salad made from nopal cactus

¡Es espectacular!—It's spectacular!

¡Es muy buen negocio!—It's very good business!

es nuestro hogar y sustento—it's our home and our livelihood

ese—dude

estoy preocupada—I'm worried

¡Fantástico!—Fantastic!

frijoles refritos y pico de gallo—refried beans and salsa of chopped tomatoes, cilantro, onion, and jalapeño

¡Fuera!—Get out!

¡Gracias!—Thank you!

habibi (when speaking to a male), habibti (when speaking to a female)—"sweetheart" or "sweetie" (Arabic); can be used like "dude" or "homes" as a way to greet a friend

hajwalah—a style of driving, like drifting, only on two wheels instead of four

han usado su creatividad—you've used your creativity

HHH!—Ha ha ha, as texted in Arabic

¡Híjole!—Jeez!, Wow!

hijos—sons

hola—hi

¡Hola! ¿Qué tal?—Hi! How's it going?

homes—short for homeboy

iguales—the same

¿Increíble, no?—Amazing, right?

insectos migratorios—migratory insects

Inshallah—God willing (Arabic)

invernadero—greenhouse

¡Ja! ¡Ja! ¡Ja!—Ha! Ha! Ha!

jardín comunitario—community garden

l'Académie des Insectes—the Academy of Insects (French)

la comunidad—the community

lakī—foolish (Arabic)

las aves—the birds

las mariposas monarca—the monarch butterflies

letrero—billboard

llantas—tires

lo siento—I'm sorry

loco—crazy, foolish

¡Los tomates!—The tomatoes!

maa'—water (Arabic)

manakeesh—Arabic flatbread topped with za'atar and ground meat

Marhaban, akhtubut!!—Hello, octopus!! (Arabic)

mercado—market

mi estrellita—my little star

mira, tú—look, you

mis amigos—my friends

mole poblano—a Mexican sauce made from poblano peppers ground up with seeds, nuts, other peppers, chocolate, and spices such as cinnamon

muchacha hermosa—beautiful woman

muchas burbujas, muchacho—lots of bubbles, dude

muchas gracias—many thanks

muy sensible—very sensitive

nada mejor que aire fresco—nothing like fresh air

nafssou—the same (Lebanese-Syrian Arabic)

No más plástico—No more plastic

¡Nunca!—Never!

Ojos de Búho—Owl Eyes

Opisthoteuthis californiana—scientific name for Flapjack Octopus

paletas heladas—Popsicles

para ocasiones especiales—for special occasions

pedos—farts

pequeño—little one; little

¡Perdóname!—Forgive me!

¡Perfecto!—Perfect!

pescaditos—little fishes

piloto—pilot

pollo asado—grilled chicken

pues . . .—well . . .

Puis-je avoir de l'eau?—May I have some water? (French)

¡Qué chido!—How cool!

¡Qué chido es poder ver!—It's so cool to be able to see!

¿Qué es esto?—What's this?

¡Qué padre!—How cool!

¿Qué pasa?—What's happening?

¡Qué triste!—How sad!

ranfla—lowrider

¡Relájate! Estamos contigo—Relax! We're with you

ridículos—ridiculous

¿Sabroso, verdad?—Tasty, right?

Salam!—Peace! (an Arabic greeting)

salsa picante—hot sauce

señor—mister

servicio para todos—service for everyone

shabashib—flip-flop (Arabic)

Shukran!—Thank you! (Arabic)

sí—yes

Sí, diga—Yes, tell me

sí, es verdad—yes, it's true

solitos—alone

solo para humanos—only for humans

súper-hiper-gigante—super-hyper-giant

tabbouleh—Arab salad made of parsley, bulgur (cracked wheat), mint, tomatoes, and sometimes cucumber, with a dressing of lemon juice and olive oil

taco—tortilla folded in half, filled with foods like vegetables, seasoned meat, and cheese

tae kwon do—Korean form of martial arts

Talavera—style of tile making originating in Islamic Spain, named for the Spanish ceramics city Talavera de la Reina and brought by Spaniards to Mexico in the 17th century

tamal—masa (cornmeal dough) containing beans or seasoned meat, wrapped in cornhusks and steamed

tan lindo—so cute

todo el mundo—everyone

¡Tranquilo!—Calm down!

tres corazones—three hearts

un marinero—a sailor

una novia—a girlfriend

¡Vámonos!—Let's go!

¡Vamos manos a la obra!—Let's get to work!

vatos—dudes, guys

vehículos—vehicles

¡Vengan!—Come on!

و—Arabic letter W, pronounced like "wow"

yallah—come on, hurry up (Arabic)

za'atar—an Arabic condiment that may include dried thyme, oregano, marjoram, toasted sesame seeds, salt, sumac, and sometimes olive oil, often served as a topping on flatbread

zatun—olive (Arabic)

AUTHOR'S NOTE

Lowriders in Space stories are all based on friends who collaborate, pooling their talents to make their dreams come true. Much like our characters, Raúl the Third and I collaborate to create our books, building our stories from our skills and our friendship.

Our Lowrider books are based on Latinx culture, and the setting reflects Raúl's hometown of El Paso/Juárez. Before this book, though, my Arab American background has been invisible. In this story I wanted to explore ways to include my culture too, especially when I discovered that just as Raúl and I merge our talents to create, our cultures have collaborated for centuries too.

I was thrilled to discover Gary Paul Nabhan's book *Arab/American: Landscape Culture, and Cuisine in Two Great Deserts*, which informed me of many commonalities between Arab American and Latinx cultures. He explains how there were several influxes of Middle Eastern immigration to the American southwest. The first was the result of the persecution of Jews and Muslims during the Spanish Inquisition in the 1500s. Later waves of immigration followed due to the conscription of Arab men into the Ottoman Empire army during World War I and the collapse of Lebanese silk production in the early 20th century. These Arab immigrants and refugees brought with them cuisine, flora, fauna, technology, art, and language, all of which then merged with the cultures of the Americas.

Translation site SpanishDict has a good list of Spanish words and their Arabic origins: https://www.spanishdict.com/guide /spanish-words-of-arabic-origin.

I'm also grateful to Rida Hamida and Benjamin Vazquez for their insight into the shared language and cuisine of Muslim and Latinx cultures, and their brilliant idea to start the movement #TacoTrucksAtEveryMosque. Taco trucks were parked near mosques, to share food and create a meeting place for Latinos and Muslims, at a time following the 2016 election when Donald Trump was persecuting both Middle Easterners and Latinx people. They created a way to inform both cultures of our similarities and to unite people in the fight for equity and social justice.

As mentioned in the story, Latinx and transplanted Middle Easterners share a lot of food culture too. For example, a Latinx food called taco al pastor—shaved pork, chiles, and onions served in a tortilla—was derived from the Middle Eastern shawarma, a roasted spit of lamb or beef, which is shaved and served in pita bread. The name taco al pastor means "in the style of the shepherd," which refers to the lamb used in the original Middle Eastern sandwich.

Hajwalah (also known as Tafheet)

Like lowriding, hotrodding, drifting, and street racing, hajwalah was invented in Saudi Arabia in the 1970s as a way to show off driving skills and cars. Cars were modified and sometimes tipped to one side so they could be driven on two wheels instead of four, often burning the rubber of the tires, sometimes even down to the metal rims. Sensationalized in films and social media, the practice spread to other Gulf states. But it also resulted in many unsafe crashes, so it is now more restricted.

Plastic and Bubble Packaging

Although plastic has been extremely useful for civilization, plastic trash is clogging up the oceans, landfills, and even ourselves! The problem with plastic is that it doesn't decompose into natural elements: it just breaks down into smaller and smaller pieces. This microplastic is now in many animals' bodies, and probably in human bodies as well. Sea animals die when they accidently ingest plastic or mistake it for food. We don't yet know all the effects of microplastics on living organisms.

We need more eco-friendly materials, and luckily, some are already being tested. Like Flappy's idea of using bubbles to hold Kooky Kola, new packaging should be biodegradable, and food packaging could even be edible, just like potato skins or ice cream cones. Edible water bottles already exist, and biodegradable straws are in the works, both designed from seaweed.

Some other possible alternative materials being researched include biodegradable plastics made from cactus juice, water-soluable packaging for materials like detergents, and edible membranes to contain liquid foods like orange juice, wine, or soup.

Researchers have recently discovered proteins in squid that could take the place of some plastics in manufacturing. These proteins are found in "teeth" in the suction cups on squids' arms and tentacles, similar to spider silk, another natural protein. But no squids need be involved; scientists can create this biodegradable material in laboratories using genetically engineered bacteria. This material also has thermal, self-healing, and electricity-conducting capabilities, which could expand the ways it could be used. A fabric with such self-healing qualities could also reduce pollution from microfibers entering the environment when the fabric is washed.

Since Lowriders books are drawn with ballpoint pens, Raúl and I wanted to share ways to recycle plastic pens and markers too. Recycle Nation explains how you can recycle pens individually or as a school or organization: www.recyclenation.com/2015/10/how-to -recycle-pens/.

Betta Fish (also known as Siamese Fighting Fish)

Male betta fish are good fathers! They build a nest of bubbles to attract females. After spawning, when the female lays eggs, the male carefully places them in the bubble nest. The male protects the nest from predators and will even rescue eggs that fall out and return them to the nest. But once the fry have hatched, the babies need to be separated from adult fish, including their fathers, who may eat them!

Monarch Butterflies and Milkweed

Every year for thousands of years, monarch butterflies have migrated from Canada and northern American states to California and Mexico. The returning butterflies also play a part in the celebration of Día de los Muertos in November, symbolizing the returning spirits of those who have died.

Since the 1990s, eastern monarchs' populations have declined by 80 percent, while California monarchs shrunk by 99.4 percent. It's heartbreaking to think that these small, plucky insects might soon go extinct because of pesticides, logging, climate change, and the lack of milkweed plants on which the butterflies rely for food. For more information, visit https://xerces.org/monarchs/.

Humans use milkweed in many ways too. During World War II, its seed fluff was used to fill life jackets (as was cattail fluff) when the war with Japan cut off the US source of kapok, another plant-based substance. Scientists also tried to use latex from milkweed sap during World War II to create rubber when there was a rubber shortage (yet another plant resource). Currently, a German company has begun producing automobile and bicycle tires made from dandelion latex to create a more sustainable product, which would take months instead of years to harvest.

Solar Cars

Right now, solar-powered cars exist, but they depend on solar cells, and it's tricky to design an aerodynamic car with cells that can draw enough power and remain affordable. Researchers are using nanotechnology to try and develop a photovoltaic (solar cell) paint. Other companies are researching technologies that would enable them to make cars that could be covered in solar paint or with a "solar cell skin."

https://opb.pbslearningmedia.org /resource/oer08.sci.phys.energy.solarpaint /solar-paint-your-roof/

https://cleantechnica.com/2016/02/08 /new-record-organic-solar-cells-today-solar-powered-car-tomorrow/

ACKNOWLEDGMENTS

A huge thank-you to Lucy Iraola, Mary Conde, Rima Karami, Nadia Boufous Phelps, Taylor Norman, Jennifer Tolo Pierce, Neil Egan, Ariela Rudy Zaltzman, and all the folks at Chronicle, and our agent, Jennifer Laughran. Thank you, Raúl III, for the years of friendship and collaboration and for using your great talent and art to share our stories! And a heartfelt thank you to Muhammad Siddiq, for his help and support with the Arabic language and the Arab cultural nuances in the book.

DEDICATIONS

For Byrd, who wanted Flappy to fall in love; for my family; and for Arabs, Latinx, Rec Centers, and mariposas everywhere. **—Cathy Camper**

This one goes out to my friend Cathy Camper. It was so much fun learning about the similarities in our cultures as I drew this book. It's been a blast working on four books with you over the past many years! **—Raúl the Third**

Library of Congress Cataloging-in-Publication Data

Names: Camper, Cathy, author. | Raúl the Third, 1976- illustrator.

Title: Lowriders to the rescue / by Cathy Camper ; illustrated by Raúl the Third.

Description: First edition. | San Francisco : Chronicle Books, 2022. | Audience: Ages 7-10. | Audience: Grades 2-3. | In English, with some Spanish words and phrases. | Summary: Lupe, an impala with a flair for mechanics, Flapjack, a sweet young octopus with vision problems, and the other Lowriders are concerned about the pollution in their town, and the greedy Upscale Business Association's plans to tear down local businesses—but first they must rescue the migrating monarchs from a wildfire caused by drought and climate change.

Identifiers: LCCN 2021018445 | ISBN 9781452179483 (hardcover) | ISBN 9781452179490 (paperback)

Subjects: LCSH: Lowriders—Comic books, strips, etc. | Lowriders—Juvenile fiction. | Climatic changes—Comic books, strips, etc. | Climatic changes—Juvenile fiction. | Wildfires—Comic books, strips, etc. | Wildfires—Juvenile fiction. | Pollution—Comic books, strips, etc. | Pollution—Juvenile fiction. | Graphic novels. | CYAC: Graphic novels. | Lowriders—Fiction. | Climatic changes—Fiction. | Wildfires—Fiction. | Pollution—Fiction. | Mexican Americans—Fiction. | Animals—Fiction. | LCGFT: Graphic novels.

Classification: LCC PZ7.7.C363 Lt 2022 | DDC 741.5/973—dc23

LC record available at https://lccn.loc.gov/2021018445

Manufactured in China.

Design by Neil J. Egan III and Jennifer Tolo Pierce.
Typeset in Comicraft Hedge Backwards, P22 Posada, and ITC Century.

10 9 8 7 6 5 4 3 2 1

Chronicle Books LLC
680 Second Street
San Francisco, California 94107

Chronicle Books—we see things differently. Become part of our community at www.chroniclekids.com.